Big Old Bones

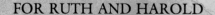

FOR RUTH AND HAROLD

Clarion Books
a Houghton Mifflin Company imprint
215 Park Avenue South, New York, NY 10003
Text copyright © 1989 by Carol Carrick
Illustrations copyright © 1989 by Donald Carrick
For information about permission to reproduce
selections from this book, write to Permissions,
Houghton Mifflin Company, 2 Park Street, Boston, MA 02108
Printed in the USA

Library of Congress Cataloging-in-Publication Data
Carrick, Carol.
Big old bones: a dinosaur tale / by Carol Carrick; illustrated
by Donald Carrick.
p. cm.
Summary: Professor Potts discovers some big old bones and puts them together in various ways
until he is satisfied he has discovered a dinosaur that once ruled the earth.
PA ISBN 0-395-61582-8   ISBN 0-89919-734-5
[1. Fossils—Fiction.] I. Carrick, Donald, ill. II. Title.
PZ7.C2344Bi 1989
[E]—dc19   88-16967
AC

HOR 10 9 8 7 6 5 4 3

Big Old Bones

A DINOSAUR TALE

by Carol Carrick
illustrated by Donald Carrick

Clarion Books
New York

Long ago, when the Old West was new, Professor Potts and his family were traveling across the country. Before their train reached the Rocky Mountains, it stopped for water.

The Professor was taking a stroll with his family when their little dog found a bone.

"Very old," said the Professor, examining the bone. "And very big. I've never seen one like it before."

He decided to stay a few days and explore.

The Professor dug till he had collected a large pile of bones.

And then he took them back East to his laboratory.

The Professor studied all the books in his
library, but none of them had bones like these.
"Hmm," he said. "It may be some kind of
giant lizard. To know for sure, I'll have to put
the bones together."

First he tried the bones this way.
"The head is too big," said the Professor.
"No one would believe an animal like this."
And too many bones were left over.

Then he tried the bones like this.

The Professor shuddered. "It gives me bad dreams," he said. "Besides, the front legs are too small."

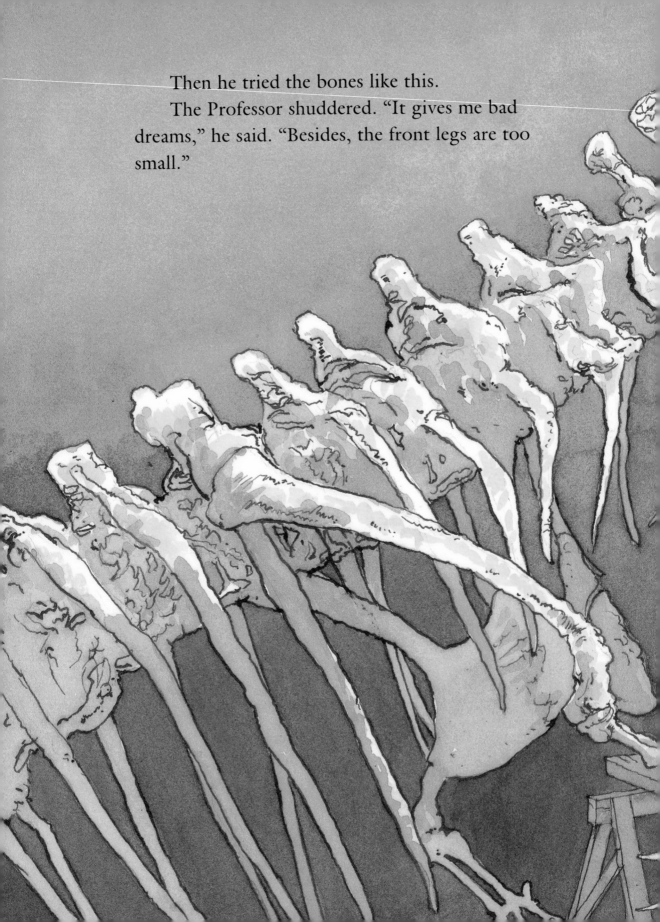

TERRIBLESAURUS
AWFULSAURUS

TYRANNOSAURUS
REX

Then the Professor tried the bones another way.
The neck was so long that he had to build a
bigger laboratory.

"Wrong again," said the Professor. "An animal this size could never walk the earth."

BRONTOSAURUS

News spread of Professor Potts's exciting work.
Reporters came to his laboratory.

But the Professor was not ready to show them his
discovery.

When the strange animal was finally put together, it still didn't look real.

"Bones are only the inside," said the Professor, so he asked his wife to make a skin for it.

At last the great day came when Professor Potts was ready to share his discovery. Important scientists arrived from all over the world.

Before he pulled aside the curtain the Professor
made a speech.

"Long ago," he said, "the earth was ruled by
a giant lizard that has never been seen before.
I have named it TRIBRONTOSAURUS REX!"

Everyone pushed forward to get the first look…

…and they were truly amazed.

MIX-UPS IN THE REAL WORLD OF SCIENCE

Fossil bones are the remains of creatures that lived long ago. In the 1800's, many people enjoyed digging them up. They were like detectives, looking for clues about the prehistoric world. Some skeletons were incomplete and the bones of many animals were often found mixed together. It was easy to make mistakes, as Professor Potts did in this story.

The first dinosaur was named in 1825. An English doctor, Gideon Mantell, called the large fossil bones and teeth his wife had discovered *Iguanodon* (Ig-wan'-o-don), which means "iguana tooth." Dr. Mantell, who made a hobby of collecting fossils, thought the large spike that formed the end of Iguanodon's thumb was a nose horn and that the creature stood on four legs, when it actually stood on two. Even the expert of his day, a French naturalist named George Cuvier, mistook the bones for those of a hippopotamus.

Edward Cope, a famous American scientist and dinosaur collector, rebuilt another dinosaur skeleton with the head on the wrong end.

In the 1870's, another American scientist, O. C. Marsh, described *Brontosaurus* from a partial skeleton. Since the skeleton had no skull, Marsh used a head found four miles from the site. This skull belonging to *Camarasaurus*, a similar dinosaur, became the generally accepted head. Even when more complete skeletons of Brontosaurus were found, casts of the wrong head were used on them until 1979, when they were finally changed.

— Carol Carrick